This book belongs to:

....

Note to parents and carers

Read it yourself is a series of classic, traditional tales, written in a simple way to give children a confident and successful start to reading.

Each book is carefully structured to include many high-frequency words that are vital for first reading. The sentences on each page are supported closely by pictures to help with reading, and to offer lively details to talk about.

The books are graded into four levels that progressively introduce wider vocabulary and longer stories as a reader's ability grows.

Ideas for use

- Begin by looking through the book and talking about the pictures. Has your child heard this story before?

- Help her with any words she does not know, either by helping her to sound them out or supplying them yourself.

- Developing readers can be concentrating so hard on the words that they sometimes don't fully grasp the meaning of what they're reading. Answering the puzzle questions on pages 30 and 31 will help with understanding.

For more information and advice, visit www.ladybird.com/readityourself

Level 2 is ideal for children who have received some reading instruction and can read short, simple sentences with help.

Special features:

Frequent repetition of main story words and phrases

Short, simple sentences

Large, clear type

Careful match between story and pictures

The king took the girl to a room full of straw.

"You must spin this straw into gold," the king said.

The girl began to cry. "I cannot do this," she said.

A funny little man came into the room.

"If you give me your necklace, I will help you," said the man.

"Yes," said the girl. "I will give you my necklace."

Educational Consultant: Geraldine Taylor

A catalogue record for this book is available from the British Library

Published by Ladybird Books Ltd
80 Strand, London, WC2R 0RL
A Penguin Company

001 - 10 9 8 7 6 5 4 3 2 1
© LADYBIRD BOOKS LTD MMXI
Ladybird, Read It Yourself and the Ladybird Logo are registered or
unregistered trade marks of Ladybird Books Limited.

ISBN: 978-1-40930-712-9

Printed in China

Rumpelstiltskin

Illustrated by Marina Le Ray

One day, a poor man took his daughter to see the king.

"My daughter can spin straw into gold," said the poor man.

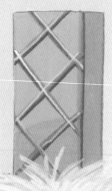

The king took the girl to a room full of straw.

"You must spin this straw into gold," the king said.

The girl began to cry. "I cannot do this," she said.

A funny little man came into the room.

"If you give me your necklace, I will help you," said the man.

"Yes," said the girl. "I will give you my necklace."

The next day, the room was full of gold.

So the king gave the girl more straw to spin into gold.

The funny little man came into the room.

"If you give me your ring, I will help you," said the funny little man.

"Yes," said the girl. "I will give you my ring."

The next day the room was full of gold.

The king gave the girl more straw. "If you can spin this straw into gold," he said, "you will be my queen."

The funny little man came into the room.

"If you give me your first child, I will help you," said the funny little man.

"Yes," said the girl. "I will give you my first child."

The next day the room was full of gold.

The king married the girl. Soon, they had a child.

The funny little man came to see the queen.

"If you cannot guess my name," said the man, "you must give me your child."

The queen began to cry.

The queen sent her men to find every name they could.

But she could not guess the name of the funny little man.

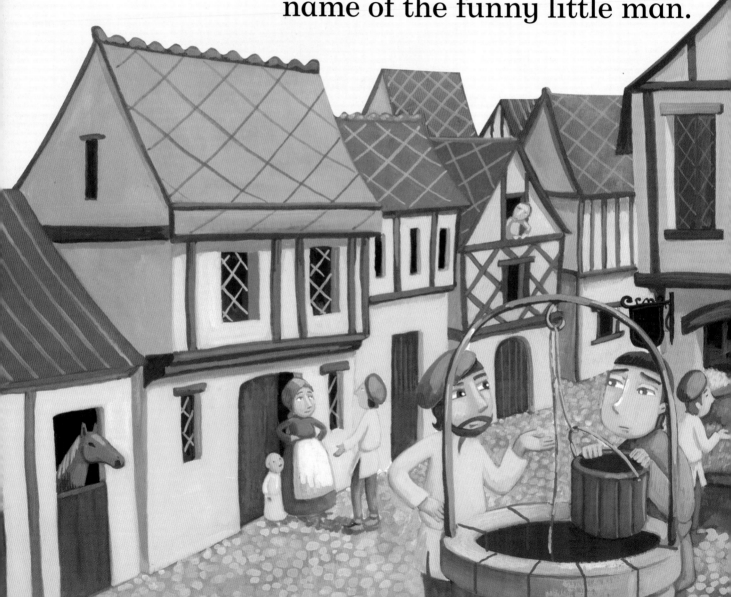

Then one man saw the
funny little man singing:

"The queen will never win my game,
For Rumpelstiltskin is my name!"

The man went to tell
the queen.

The next day the queen said to the funny little man, "Is your name... Rumpelstiltskin?"

And the funny little man was so cross, he ran away and was never seen again.

How much do you remember about the story of Rumpelstiltskin? Answer these questions and find out!

- What did the poor man say the girl could do?

- Who helped her to do this?

- Can you name two things the girl gave the funny little man?

- How did the queen find out Rumpelstiltskin's name?

Look at the pictures and match them to the story words.

gold

king

straw

girl

Rumpelstiltskin

Read it yourself
with Ladybird

The Three Billy Goats Gruff

Cinderella

Little Red Hen

Goldilocks and the Three Bears

The Enormous Turnip

The Magic Porridge Pot

The Ugly Duckling

The Emperor's New Clothes

The Gingerbread Man

Sleeping Beauty

Little Red Riding Hood

Town Mouse and Country Mouse

Sly Fox and Red Hen

The Three Little Pigs

Chicken Licken

Rumpelstiltskin

The Elves and the Shoemaker

Jack and the Beanstalk

Hansel and Gretel

Rapunzel

The Pied Piper of Hamelin

The Wizard of Oz

Heidi

Snow White and the Seven Dwarfs

Collect all the titles in the series.